Disney Vampirina

SCARE B and B

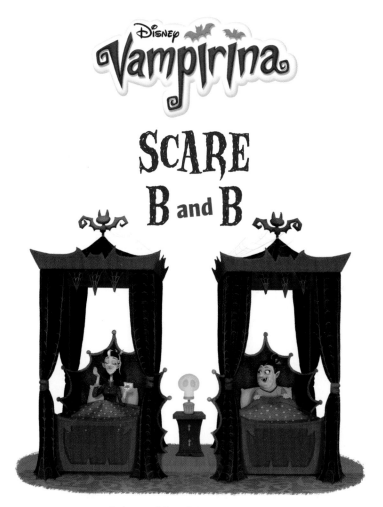

Adapted by **Chelsea Beyl**

Based on the episode written by **Jeff King**

Illustrated by **Imaginism Studio** and the **Disney Storybook Art Team**

Disney PRESS

Los Angeles • New York

First Paperback Edition, August 2017   10 9 8 7 6 5 4 3 2 1
ISBN 978-1-368-00965-2
FAC-029261-17195
Library of Congress Control Number: 2017942226

Printed in the United States of America
For more Disney Press fun, visit www.disneybooks.com

SUSTAINABLE
FORESTRY
INITIATIVE

ertified Sourcing
www.sfiprogram.org
SFI-01415

This is Vampirina.
Her friends call her Vee.

This is Vee's house.

It is also a Scare B and B.

A Scare B and B is a house that is like a hotel. Monsters can come and stay.

Vee helps her mom decorate.

Vee's mom posts the Scare B and B
on the World Wide Cobweb.

The doorbell shrieks. It must be their first guest!

It is not a monster guest.
It is Edna, Edgar, and Poppy.
Their house is being painted.
They need a place to stay.

Poppy knows Vee is a vampire.
Edna and Edgar do not.
They could get spooked!

"Edna and Edgar can stay in the guest room," says Vee. "Poppy can stay with me!"

Vampire sisters show up next.

They do not want to stay with humans.
They want to stay at a Scare B and B.

Now the Hauntleys have humans and vampires but only one room. What will they do?

Vee says, "Humans sleep at night.
Vampires sleep all day. We will
keep them apart. It will be okay."

The vampires are ready for bed.
Poppy's family leaves.
Vee brings the sisters in.

The sisters find Edna's slippers.
"We hope there are no humans here,"
they say.

The vampire sisters get ready for bed. They brush their fangs.

They put green frog slime on
their faces.

Edgar goes upstairs.
He forgot his phone.
What if Edgar sees the vampires?

Vee zooms into the room.
She shuts the bed curtains.

Vee goes batty and swoops out.
Edgar does not see the vampires.

Vee's mom makes lunch for her
human guests.

One of the sisters flies into the
kitchen! She wants a bedtime snack.

Vee throws flour in the air.
The flour hides everyone!
The humans do not see the bat.
The bat does not see the humans.

That night, the sisters wake up.
Vee takes them for a flight.
Now Edna and Edgar can go to sleep.

Later Vee and Poppy hear Edna's voice downstairs.

They hear vampire voices, too!

They run to the kitchen.
Edna looks like a monster!
She chats with the sisters.

"The vampires think your mom
is like them!" says Vee.
"And now they are friends!"
says Poppy.

The next day, Edna thanks the Hauntleys.
"I liked meeting those sisters, too," she says.

"It looks like vampires and
humans can be friends," says Poppy.
"Just like us!"